For Dave
H.B.

To my Africa Dad, Ken Senior
M.S.

Consultant:
Andrew Durham BSc (Hons)
Deputy Team Leader, Elephant Team, Whipsnade Zoo

First American edition published in 2008
by Boxer Books Limited.

Distributed in the United States and Canada by
Sterling Publishing Co., Inc.
387 Park Avenue South, New York, NY 10016-8810

First published in Great Britain in 2008
by Boxer Books Limited.
www.boxerbooks.com

ISBN 13: 978-1-905417-75-9   ISBN 10: 1-905417-75-6

1 3 5 7 9 10 8 6 4 2

Printed in China

All of our papers are sourced from managed forests and renewable resources.

ELEPHANT'S STORY

WRITTEN BY HARRIET BLACKFORD

ILLUSTRATED BY MANJA STOJIC

BOXER BOOKS

Elephant is born on the vast African savanna, a tiny wrinkly baby with big floppy ears and a most extraordinary nose. She is tiny to her mother, but really, she is a very big baby.

Her mother's huge solid legs stand on either side of Elephant's body, protecting her as the baby tests her wobbly legs.

Elephant's mother uses her trunk to stroke her new baby all over. Then there are many trunks stroking and touching her. All around Elephant, tall legs seem to stretch up to the sky and long trunks hang down as the herd greets the new arrival.

It is not long before Elephant is charging around her mother, flapping her ears to frighten the birds in the grass and playing with the other youngsters in the herd.

The grown-ups in Elephant's herd are all part of her family—
aunts, sisters, cousins, and grandmother. When danger
threatens, all the grown-ups protect the young ones.

Soon Elephant has to learn to control her trunk. It is hard work to get it to go where she wants. Sucking up water to squirt into her mouth is very tricky.

Elephant uses her trunk to take food from her mother's mouth. She tries to put it into her own mouth without dropping it.

The big old grandmother elephant leads
the herd to the watering hole. This is
the best place in the world!

Elephant squirts water over her back and wallows in the muddy water to cool off.

The herd starts to leave the waterhole.
But Elephant wants to eat one more juicy
tuft of grass. The grass is so tough,
she has to pull and pull.

Suddenly her feet slip on the muddy bank and Elephant tumbles back into the water. The bank is high and she cannot see her mother. For the first time in her life, she is alone. Elephant squeals with fright.

Then a big strong trunk wraps around her tummy and
another one wraps around her trunk. The grown-ups
pull her out of the water . . .

and she lands in the mud with a plop!
Elephant's mother strokes her baby all over
to help her feel safe again.

Time passes, and Elephant is growing taller and bigger. Her mother has a new baby now, and Elephant helps keep watch over it. She is especially careful at the waterhole!

Elephant is hungry. The grass is dry and the trees are bare of green leaves. For a long time there has been no rain. The big old grandmother leads the herd far away to a lush green field with a fence around it.

The biggest elephants break down the fence,
and all the hungry elephants start eating.

All of a sudden, the farmer
appears in a big noisy car.
He drives toward the herd,
blowing his horn, to
frighten the elephants
away from his field.

Elephant rushes through
the fence, but the ground
is so dry that the air is
soon full of dust.
She cannot even see
where she is going!

Elephant cannot see the new baby elephant, but she can hear its frightened squeals. Elephant goes back to the fence, flapping her great big ears. She calls to the baby to come to her. Then she leads it away to join the rest of the herd.

The herd stands close together.
They link their trunks to greet
Elephant and the new baby.

Now Elephant strokes the baby
with her trunk, just as the
grown-ups do. It is good to
be back in the safety of the
herd once more.

Elephants

A note from the author

Elephants learn to take care of themselves as they grow up, just as children do. And they take a long time to learn what they need to know to survive as an adult. This book tells the story of one baby elephant on the African savanna who grows up to be a responsible member of her herd.

Here are some facts about elephants: Elephants are the biggest land animals alive today. A grown-up male elephant weighs as much as eighty people and can be twice as tall as a full-grown person! Elephants have an amazing nose called a trunk. The trunk is formed from their top lip and nose, which grows very long and very strong. Elephants have big ears they can spread out in the breeze to keep themselves cool. Their legs are like tree trunks. Their front teeth, called tusks, are very long and stick out of their mouths. In fact, most things about elephants are big.

Elephants are mammals - which means they have hair - but they have only a sparse covering of hair on their bodies. Elephants can live a long time; some live to be about sixty years old in the wild.

There are three types of elephant: the Asian elephant, the African savanna elephant, and the African forest elephant. The Asian elephant lives in India and other parts of Asia and has smaller ears, one "finger" at the end of its trunk and only the males have tusks. The African savanna and forest elephants have two "fingers" and the end of their trunks. The forest elephant is smaller than the savanna elephant and its tusks point downwards rather than curve up. The savanna elephant is the biggest of all, with huge ears and long tusks. A female elephant is fully grown up at about ten years old. She has one calf at a time every three to five years. The females live together in herds, led by the oldest female, called the matriarch. The females are all related. They get to know each other very well. Male elephants leave the herd in their late teenage years. They live with other males in small groups or stay on their own for a while.

The elephant is an endangered species, which means there are not as many of them as there used to be. Elephants are hunted for their ivory tusks, which are highly valued. Farmers also hunt elephants to keep them off their lands. People still kill elephants, but their biggest problem is the spread of roads, towns, and farms across their natural habitat. They need protection in special habitats set aside just for them or they will disappear altogether. Perhaps you, too, can help protect the elephants.